W9-BTI-183

BUBBLE TROUBLE

○

BUBBLE TROUBLE

& Other Poems and Stories

written and illustrated by

Margaret Mahy

MARGARET K. MCELDERRY BOOKS
New York
Maxwell Macmillan International
New York   Oxford   Singapore   Sydney

Margaret K. McElderry Books
Macmillan Publishing Company
866 Third Avenue, New York, NY 10022

Macmillan Publishing Company is part of the
Maxwell Communication Group of Companies.

2   4   6   8   10   9   7   5   3   1

Library of Congress Cataloging-in-Publication Data
Mahy, Margaret.   Bubble trouble, and other poems and stories / written
and illustrated by Margaret Mahy. — 1st United States ed.   p.   cm.
Summary: A collection of humorous stories and poems featuring a baby flying
in a bubble, a lovestruck crocodile, and a grandmother who is tired of winter.
ISBN 0-689-50557-4
1. Children's literature, New Zealand.   [1. Literature—Collections.
2. Humorous poetry.   3. Humorous stories.]   I. Title.
PZ7.M2773Bu 1992   [Fic]—dc20   92-3540

To all the cousins—
Luke and Jack,
and Arthur and Giles

◯

Contents

○

BUBBLE TROUBLE

○

Bubble Trouble

O

Little Mabel blew a bubble and it caused a lot of
   trouble—
Such a lot of bubble trouble in a bibble-bobble way.
For it broke away from Mabel as it bobbed across the
   table,
Where it bobbled over Baby, and it wafted him away.

The baby didn't quibble. He began to smile and
   dribble,
For he liked the wibble-wobble of the bubble in the
   air.

But Mabel ran for cover as the bubble bobbed above
  her,
And she shouted out for Mother, who was putting up
  her hair.

At the sudden cry of trouble, Mother took off at the
  double,
For the squealing left her reeling...made her terrified
  and tense,
Saw the bubble for a minute, with the baby bobbing in
  it,
As it bibbled by the letterbox and

                          bobbed across the fence.

In her garden, Chrysta Gribble had begun to cry and
    cavil
At her lazy brother, Greville, reading novels in his
    bed.
But she bellowed, "Gracious, Greville!" and she
    groveled on the gravel,
When the baby in the bubble
    bibble-bobbled overhead.

In a garden folly, Tybal, and his jolly mother, Sybil,

Sat and played a game of Scrabble, shouting shrilly as
they scored.

But they both began to babble and to scrobble with the
Scrabble

As the baby in the bubble bibble-bobbled by the board.

Then crippled Mr. Copple and his wife (a crabby
couple),

Set out arm in arm to hobble and to squabble down
the lane.

But the baby in the bubble turned their hobble to a
joggle

As they raced away
like rockets...
and they've never
limped again.

Even feeble Mrs. Threeble
   in a muddle with her
   needle
(Matching pink and purple
   patches for a pretty
   patchwork quilt),
When her older sister told her, tossed the quilt across
   her shoulder,
As she set off at a totter in her tattered tartan kilt.

At the shops a busy rabble, met to gossip and to
  gabble,
Started gibbering and goggling as the bubble bobbled
  by.
Mother, hand in hand with Mabel, flew as fast as she
  was able,
Full of trouble lest the bubble burst or vanish in the
  sky.

After them came Greville Gribble in his nightshirt,
  with his novel
(All about a haunted hovel) held on high above his
  head,
Followed by his sister, Chrysta (though her boots had
  made a blister),

Then came Tybal, pulling Sybil, with the Scrabble for a
   sled.

After them the Copple couple came cavorting at the
   double,
Then a jogger (quite a slogger) joined the crowd who
   called and coughed.
Up above the puzzle people—and toward the chapel
   steeple—
Rose the bubble (with the baby) slowly lifting up aloft.

There was such a flum-a-diddle (Mabel huddled in the
   middle),
Canon Dapple left the chapel, followed
   by the chapel choir.

And the treble singer, Abel, threw an apple core at
    Mabel,
As the baby in the bubble bobbled up a little higher.

Oh, they giggled and they goggled until all their brains
    were boggled,
As the baby in the bubble rose above the little town.
"With the problem let us grapple," murmured kindly
    Canon Dapple,
"And the problem we must grapple with is bringing
    Baby down."

"Now, let Mabel stand on Abel, who could stand in
    turn on Tybal,
Who could stand on Greville Gribble, who could stand
    upon the wall,
While the people from the shop'll stand to catch them
    if they topple,
Then perhaps they'll reach the bubble, saving Baby
    from a fall."
But Abel, though a treble, was a rascal and a rebel,
Fond of getting into trouble when he didn't have to
    sing.
Pushing quickly through the people, Abel clambered
    up the steeple
With nefarious intentions and a pebble in his sling!

Abel quietly aimed the pebble past the steeple of the
    chapel,
At the baby in the bubble wibble-wobbling way up
    there.
And the pebble *burst* the bubble! So the future seemed
    to fizzle
For the baby boy who grizzled as he tumbled through
    the air.

What a moment for a mother as her infant plunged
    above her!

There were groans and gasps and gargles from the
   horror-stricken crowd.

Sybil said, "Upon my honor, *there's* a baby who's a
   goner!"

And Chrysta hissed with emphasis, "It shouldn't be
   allowed!"

But Mabel, Tybal, Greville, and the jogger (christened
   Neville)

Didn't quiver, didn't quaver, didn't drivel, shrivel, wilt.

But as one they made a swivel, and with action (firm
   but civil),

They divested Mrs. Threeble of her pretty patchwork
   quilt.

Oh, what calculated catchwork! Baby bounced into the
   patchwork,

Where his grizzles turned to giggles and to wriggles of
   delight!

And the people stared dumbfounded, as he bobbled
and rebounded,
Till the baby boy was grounded and his mother held
him tight.

And the people there still prattle—there is lots of
tittle-tattle—
For they glory in the story, young and old folk, gold
and gray,
Of how wicked treble Abel tripled trouble with his
pebble,
But how Mabel (and some others) saved her brother
and the day.

The Runaway
Reptiles

O

Sir Hamish Hawthorn, the famous old explorer, was not happy.

"Oh, Marilyn," he cried to his favorite niece. "I long to go exploring up the Orinoco River once more, but who will look after my pets?"

"The Reverend Crabtree next door will feed the cats, I'm sure," said Marilyn. "He is a very kind-hearted man. And I will take care of the alligator for you."

"But, Marilyn," Sir Hamish said, "what about your neighbor? He might object to alligators."

Marilyn lived in Marigold Avenue—a most respectable street. The house next door was exactly the same
as hers. It had the same green front door, the same
garden, and the same marigolds. A man called Archie
Lightfoot lived there. He was rather handsome, but
being handsome was not everything. Would he enjoy
having a twenty-foot Orinoco alligator next door?

"Don't worry, Uncle dear," said Marilyn. "I shall
work something out."

At that exact moment, by a curious coincidence,
Archie Lightfoot was opening an important-looking
letter. He read:

Dear Mr. Lightfoot,
Your great-aunt—who died last week—has
left you her stamp album, full of rare and
valuable stamps.

"Terrific!" shouted Archie. Though he had never met his great-aunt, he had inherited her great love of stamps. Now, it seemed, he had inherited her stamp album as well. He read on eagerly.

There is one condition. You must give a good
home to your aunt's twenty-foot Nile croco-
dile. If you refuse, you don't get the stamp
collection. Those are the terms of the will.

"What will Marilyn Hawthorn say?" muttered Archie Lightfoot. "A beautiful girl like that will not want a twenty-foot Nile crocodile on the lawn next door. I will have to work something out."

That night, Marilyn Hawthorn tossed and turned. She could not sleep. In the end she decided to get up and make herself some toast. She could see the light next door shining on the marigolds. Archie Lightfoot was evidently having something to eat as well.

There is something about midnight meals that
makes people have clever ideas. Sure enough, on the
stroke of twelve, Marilyn Hawthorn suddenly thought
of the answer to her problem.

The next day she made a large blue sunbonnet and a
pretty shawl on her sewing machine, and borrowed
the biggest motorized wheelchair she could find. Then
she went around to her uncle's house.

Before leaving for the Orinoco, Uncle Hamish
helped his niece settle the alligator comfortably in the
wheelchair, packing it in with lots of wet cushions.

The big sunbonnet nearly hid its snout, but Marilyn
made it wear sunglasses to help the disguise.

"I shan't forget this," Sir Hamish said in a deeply grateful voice.

"Neither shall I," murmured Marilyn, wheeling the alligator out into the street.

As Marilyn pushed the disguised alligator through her front gate she noticed Archie Lightfoot pushing a large motorized wheelchair through his front gate, too. Sitting in it was someone muffled in a scarf, a floppy hat, and sunglasses.

"My old grandfather is coming to live with me for a while," Archie said with a nervous laugh.

"How funny!" said Marilyn. "My old granny is coming to stay with *me*."

The two old grandparents looked at each other through their sunglasses and grinned toothily.

"Unfortunately," Archie added quickly, "my old grandfather can sometimes be very crabby. He has a big heart, but occasionally he works himself up into a bad temper. Do warn your grandmother not to talk to him."

"I have the same problem with Granny," Marilyn replied. "She is basically bighearted, but at times she can be bad-tempered. If you try to talk to her when she's hungry, she just snaps your head off!"

At first, things went smoothly. Every day Marilyn gave the alligator a large breakfast of fish and tomato sauce. Then she tucked the huge reptile into the wheelchair with blankets soaked in homemade mud. Next, she wheeled it into the garden and settled it down with a bottle of cordial, an open can of sardines and the newspaper. The alligator always looked eagerly over the fence to see what was going on next door.

In his garden, Archie Lightfoot was settling his old grandfather down with tunafish sandwiches and an automobile magazine. His grandfather blew a daring kiss to Marilyn Hawthorn's grandmother. Marilyn saw her alligator blow one back.

"You are not to blow kisses to a respectable old gentleman," she said sternly. The grandfather blew another kiss and the alligator did the same. Marilyn smacked its paw. It tried to bite her, but she was much too quick for it.

While Marilyn Hawthorn and Archie Lightfoot were at work, the two old grandparents blew kisses to one another and tossed fishy snacks across the fence.

That evening, when Marilyn Hawthorn got home, she noticed that her alligator seemed rather ill. It sighed a great deal, and merely toyed with its sardines

at supper. Marilyn felt its forehead. It was warm and
feverish, a bad thing in alligators, which are, of course,
cold-blooded. She took it to the vet at once.

"What on earth is this?" cried the vet, listening to
the alligator's heart. "This alligator is in love!"

The alligator sighed so deeply it accidentally
swallowed the vet's thermometer.

It must be homesick for the Orinoco, Marilyn
thought to herself. So she took a day off work,
wrapped cool mud-packs around the alligator, and put
it in the marigold garden—with a large photograph of
the Orinoco River to look at.

As she was doing this, Archie Lightfoot's face appeared over the garden fence.

"Oh, I'm so worried about my grandfather," he cried. "I have had to take him to the vet—I mean, the doctor—and he sighed so deeply that he swallowed a stethoscope."

"And I've had to take the day off work to look after my old granny," said Marilyn. "*She* has swallowed a thermometer."

"Ahem!" Archie Lightfoot coughed, clearing his throat nervously. "Perhaps, since you are taking the day off work, you might like to slip over and see my stamp collection."

"I'd love to," replied Marilyn.

Marilyn Hawthorn and Archie Lightfoot spent rather a long time looking at the stamp collection.

They forgot their responsibilities. When they switched on the radio, they were alarmed to hear the following announcement:

"We interrupt this program to bring you horrifying news. Two twenty-foot saurians— crocodiles, or perhaps they are alligators— both wearing sunglasses, are driving down the main road in motorized wheelchairs."

"Oh, no!" cried Archie Lightfoot.
"Oh, no!" cried Marilyn Hawthorn. Together, they ran outside. Their two lawns were quite empty.
"This is serious," gasped Marilyn. "Oh, Mr.

Lightfoot, I must confess that my grandmother is really an alligator!"

"And my old grandfather's a crocodile," cried Archie. "I didn't dream that a lovely woman like you could be fond of reptiles."

"We can discuss that later," said Marilyn briskly. "First, we must get our dear pets back."

Quickly, they climbed into Marilyn's sports car and took off after the runaway reptiles. They soon saw them whizzing along in their wheelchairs. Overhead, a police helicopter hovered, with several police officers and the vet inside it.

"It's very strange," said Marilyn, "but they seem to be heading for my uncle's house. I do wish Uncle Hamish were at home. He would know what to do in a case like this."

The runaways turned into the street where Marilyn's uncle lived, but they did not turn in at his gate. Instead, they went through the next-door gateway, straight to the home of the Reverend Crabtree.

Imagine Marilyn's surprise when she saw her Uncle Hamish sitting on the veranda, showing the Reverend Crabtree his souvenirs of the Orinoco.

"Uncle, I didn't know you were back!" she exclaimed.

"Well, I have only just returned," he said, looking in amazement at the two reptiles. "The Orinoco wasn't as good as I remembered it, so I came home early. But, Marilyn, why has my alligator split itself in two?"

"Oh, Uncle, this is not another alligator—it's a crocodile. And it belongs to Archie Lightfoot," Marilyn explained. "These two bad reptiles ran away together in their wheelchairs and came here."

By now the police helicopter had landed on the lawn, and the police officers, followed by the vet, came running over.

"Don't hurt those saurians," the vet was shouting. "They are not very well. They are in love!"

"Ah," said the Reverend Crabtree. "I understand! They have eloped and wish to get married."

The crocodile and the alligator swished their tails and snapped their jaws as one reptile, to show he was right.

"I'm not sure if I, a minister of the church, should marry an alligator and a crocodile," said the Reverend Crabtree doubtfully. "It doesn't seem very respectable."

"But it seems a pity to miss out on the chance of marrying two creatures so clearly in love," said Archie. Then, turning to Marilyn he added, "Suppose we get married, too. Will that make it more respectable?

After all, we did bring these two reptiles together. It's only fair that they should do the same for us!"

So Marilyn Hawthorn married Archie Lightfoot, and the crocodile and the alligator were married too. Sir Hamish gave both brides away. Then he swapped over and became best man to the two bridegrooms.

Marilyn and Archie turned their two little houses into one large house, and their lawns into a swimming pool for the two saurians. And they lived happily ever after, even though they had to begin every morning of their lives together feeding sardines to a handsome Nile crocodile and an Orinoco alligator—both with big hearts and even bigger appetites.

Hiccups

O

Oh, horrors! Look at Mother! She is slamming down
   the phone.
Through her lips there comes a mumble and a
   melancholy moan.
"Oh, what has happened, Mother? You have turned a
   ghastly gray.
What!!! Granny's on her bicycle and racing on her
   way!"
Just when Baby's got the hiccups!

Goodness gracious guzzleguts! Oh, gilly-golly-gosh!

Quickly! Hide the dirty dishes that we haven't time to wash.

Brush the cat hair off the cushions! Vacuum up the crusts and crumbs!

Let's be looking trim and tidy by the time our granny comes!

Curses! Baby's got the hiccups.

We must tidy, tidy, tidy now that Granny's on the way.

She has not been back to see us since that fatal Christmas Day

When she slipped on Lily's skateboard, crashing down upon the cat,

31

While the dog devoured her knitting and her handbag
  and her hat.
And now Baby's got the hiccups!

Go and bring the children inside. Fetch them in and
  sponge them down,
For Granny's on her bicycle and rocketing through
  town.
And she likes a house that's tidy.... Wipe those soup
  stains off the floor!
We must one and all be perfect by the time she's at
  the door.
But Baby's still got hiccups!

Jack's busy playing football. He is racing for a goal,

When Mum runs in and tackles him. The coach cries,
"Bless my soul!"

He quickly tries to sign her up. He likes her forward
play,

But football counts for nothing when your granny's on
the way.

And Baby's got the hiccups!

So Jack is washed behind the ears and made to change
   his shirt,
Though he is not the only one rejoicing in the dirt.
There's Father in the garden looking like a Brussels
   sprout,
But Mum is quite relentless and she quickly weeds him
   out.
Listen! Baby still has hiccups.
Now, Lily, run and fetch the twins from underneath
   the shed.
Oh! They're burrowing like rabbits and they're mud
   from toe to head.

We must swishy-swishy-swash them. We must rub-a-
dub them clean,
Crying, "Giddy goats and griffins! Granny's racing to
the scene!"
And Baby's got the hiccups! What a time to get the
hiccups!

We are trembling, we are tidy, we are starched and
stuck in place.
We are standing feet together; there is fear on every
face.
For our granny is approaching. She is at the corner
now

When the dog commences howling, and he wrinkles
   up his brow.
How can we stop the hiccups?

Oh, Baby is a darling, but the hiccups...What a shame!
If she hiccups at our granny, we are bound to get the
   blame!
Oh, her hiccups shake the kitchen. It is getting much
   too much.
She is rattling all the saucepans and the silverware and
   such.
Such a bad attack of hiccups!

How do you cure the hiccups? "Give the kid a fright!"
   cries Jack.
"Once you're frightened, hiccups vanish, and they say
   they don't come back!"

Let us terrify the baby! Let us roar like crocodiles!
But Baby only hiccups in between her sunny smiles.
For she didn't *mind* her hiccups.

Let us try a drink of water. That is sure to do the trick.
And Baby drank the water, then she hiccupped and
   was sick!
So we had to change her sweater and her diaper and
   dress.
And she giggled and she gurgled and she hiccupped
   through the mess—
When our baby had the hiccups.

"We are doomed to harbor hiccups," Father yells in
   deep despair.

"It is destiny!" moans Mother, falling backward in her
   chair.
But Baby laughs and hiccups—yes, she hiccups and she
   grins
At her mother and her father, Jack and Lily, and the
   twins.
She rather likes her hiccups!

Oh, look! The door is open. Look! There's Gran
   arrived, at last.
Is she going to forgive us for that fatal Christmas
   past?
She has bought another handbag. She has bought a
   brand-new hat,
Which alarms the dog (and Father) and which terrifies
   the cat!
Just when Baby's got the hiccups!

"Give the child to me!" cries Granny.
   "I am old enough to know
That the proper kind of cuddle
   often makes the
   hiccups go!

Though your dog once ate my handbag, that's a long
    way in the past...
If the oldest hugs the youngest then the
    hiccups cannot last."
Even very stubborn hiccups!

Granny hugs our darling baby and she kisses Baby's
    head.

And then Baby stops her hiccups, doing just what
    Granny said.
"I am getting old," says Granny. "I am nearly ninety-
    three.
So now I've solved the problem, may I have a cup of
    tea?
And we'll overlook the hiccups!"

Bring her tea and bring her biscuits! Bring a slice of
    Lily's cake!
Yes, but should we let her eat it? Could it be a bad
    mistake?
"It's been lovely," mumbles Granny, "and we've had a
    lovely talk."
Then... *Hiccup! Hiccup! Hiccup!* rattles every spoon
    and fork.
Now *Granny* has the hiccups!

Then Lily laughs, and Jack laughs too—the twins
    laugh even more.
And Mum begins to giggle, whereas Father starts to
    roar!
And Baby grins and gurgles (though her laugh is very
    small),
While Granny hic-hic-hiccups, laughing loudest of
    us all.

The Gargling Gorilla

O

Rosa Sungrove, the well-known animal lover, was going out for the evening, so she needed someone brave and kind to feed all her pets. Tim, who lived next door, agreed to help her.

"Are you brave?" she asked him.

"Very brave," said Tim. "I'm not afraid of spiders or sharks or alligators. But I'm very kind too."

"Good," said Rosa. "You sound just the one to look after my pets. Now, let me explain. The cat likes cat snacks and the cat-snack pack is in the tall cupboard.

The tall cupboard is beside the fridge, and the fridge is over there, on the other side of the sink. Right?"

"Right!" said Tim.

"However, when the vulture sees the cat being fed he often gets a little peckish, and I don't want a peckish vulture around the place. The vulture chunks are *inside* the fridge (over there on the other side of the sink). They are in the blue bowl. Right?"

"Right!" said Tim cheerfully.

The vulture looked down from its perch and clacked its beak. Tim smiled at it. He was not afraid of vultures.

"The wolfhound is outside under the camellia," Rosa went on. "When she smells the vulture chunks, she gets very hungry. Her doggie crunch is in the little

cupboard *this* side of the sink, but her dish is on the
bottom shelf of the tea wagon beside the fridge over
there on the *other* side of the sink. She *must* have her
dish or she gets nasty. It's not her fault. She just does.
Right?"

"Right!" Tim agreed.

"When the giant chinchilla rabbit hears the rattle of
the doggie crunch being poured into the dog bowl, it
often thinks it's hearing rabbit nibble being poured
into the rabbit dish, and comes rushing inside.
Chinchilla rabbits are mostly gentle, but this is a *giant*

chinchilla rabbit," Rosa warned Tim. "If you don't feed her she will try to bounce on you, and she is dangerously heavy. The rabbit dish is the red one on the top shelf of the tea wagon, there beside the fridge on the other side of the sink. And the actual rabbit nibbles are in the large economy-sized purple package on top of the fridge.

"And when you have finished feeding the animals you might like a little refreshment yourself. The tea is

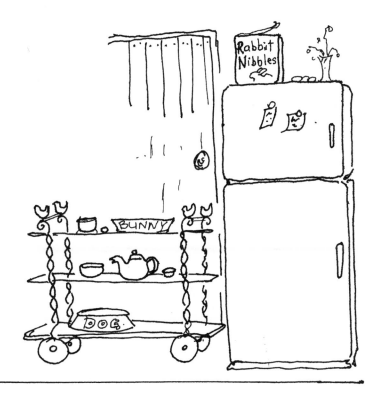

in the yellow jar at the end of the shelf on the other side of the sink. The bread box is next to the yellow jar. The butter and cheese are in the fridge, and crackers are in the green box. Good luck! And now, I must go." But at the door Rosa stopped. "Oh, by the way," she called, "the gorilla is in the cupboard *under* the sink."

The gorilla! In the cupboard under the sink!

Of course, most people know that gorillas are gentle and retiring, but Tim was unaware of this. The very

bravest people can be scared of at least one thing, and Tim, though brave about absolutely everything else, happened to be scared of gorillas.

When I took on this job, he thought to himself, I did not know a gorilla was involved.

At that moment something in the cupboard under the sink began to gurgle, or perhaps to gargle. However, a gargling gorilla is just as scary as a gurgling one.

Tim made up his mind to keep away from the cupboard under the sink in case the gorilla put out a hairy hand and grabbed him as he was going by. But it wasn't easy, for the sink, and the cupboard under the sink, were in the very middle of the kitchen.

First, he fed the cat. He took the fireplace tongs and tied the tong handles to the handles of the broom and the mop. Then he reached over and, after several tries, opened the tall cupboard beside the fridge and sucked out the cat-snack pack with the vacuum cleaner. Then he lightly spiked the cat-snack pack with a fork tied to the handle of the thing you use to wash high-up

windows, twisting it over so cleverly that the cat's dish was soon filled with delicious cat snacks. The cat didn't seem to be at all frightened of the gorilla. It ate its dinner right in front of the cupboard under the sink.

When the vulture saw the cat was getting something, it stretched its neck greedily and flapped its wings. Tim did not want to walk past the cupboard under the sink in case the gorilla put out a hairy hand and grabbed an ankle. On the other hand, the poor vulture was certainly rather hungry. It began staring at the cat with a sinister expression. Being kind, Tim just had to feed it. First, he used the tongs to reach past the sink to open the fridge. Then he took the thing you use to wash high-up windows (which still had the fork tied to the end of it) and he reached *into* the blue bowl inside the fridge. He spiked the vulture chunks one by one, passing them (on the end of the fork) up to the vulture on its perch. The vulture gobbled them down, clacking its beak with happiness in between the gobbles.

The smell of the vulture chunks brought the
wolfhound in from the veranda. Her doggie crunch
was easy to reach, but when Tim tried to give it to her
in a china soup tureen instead of her dish, she turned
nasty and started snapping her teeth. She couldn't help
it. Her dish was on the bottom shelf of the tea wagon
beside the fridge on the other side of the cupboard
under the sink with the gorilla gurgling (or gargling)
inside it.

The wolfhound saw Tim was hesitating. She put her
giant paws on his shoulders and began slapping his
face with a tongue like a wet carpet. It showed him
just how sharp her teeth were: They were very sharp!

The tongs would not reach quite as far as the
wolfhound's dish. Fortunately, a fishing line that had
belonged to Rosa's uncle was over the fireplace in the

sitting room. Tim quickly cast the hook over the edge of the dish, reeled it in and filled it with doggie crunch. Soon the whole kitchen rattled with the sound of the wolfhound crunching, the vulture clacking its beak, the cat snacking on cat-snacks, and the gorilla gargling under the sink.

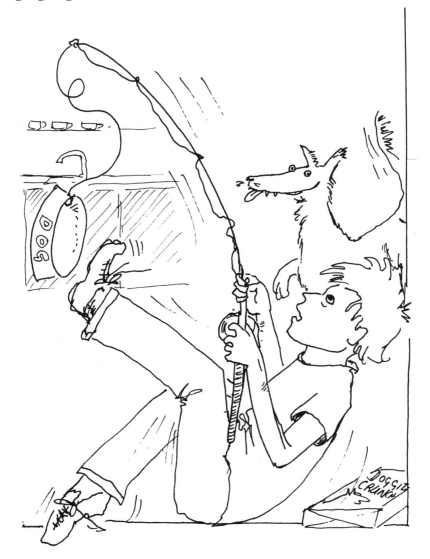

Tim was about to relax a little when the giant chinchilla rabbit came bounding in. It was a very big rabbit indeed. It made nibbling noises and looked hungry. Tim was so kindhearted that he couldn't stand it, and he wanted to help. But it wasn't easy. He cast with his line again, pulled the tea wagon over, retrieved the red rabbit dish, picked up the tongs, and reached over and got the rabbit nibbles down from the

top of the fridge. *Gargle-gargle* went the gorilla under the sink, furious because Tim had been too clever for it.

When Rosa arrived home a moment later she found the rabbit nibbling, the wolfhound crunching, the vulture clacking, the cat snacking, and the disappointed gorilla gargling. The mop and the broom and the thing used for washing high-up windows were in their right places, the tongs were beside the fireplace, and the fishing line was back over the mantelpiece.

"How well you've done!" she cried. "You are obviously brave *and* kind."

"The only one I haven't fed is the gorilla," said Tim apologetically.

"The gorilla?" exclaimed Rosa.

"The gorilla in the cupboard under the sink," explained Tim.

"Oh!" said Rosa. She began to laugh. She opened the cupboard under the sink. "This is what I keep in the cupboard under the sink," she said. "The *griller*! It's for grilling cheese on toast. I just thought you might like some cheese on toast for your supper."

"But I heard it gargling," Tim said.

"Oh, those are just pipes leading to the sink," said Rosa. "They do gargle a bit."

The pipes gurgled as she spoke, and the back door opened.

"Do you mean there isn't a gorilla after all?" asked Tim. The back door shut.

"Oh, there *is* a gorilla," said Rosa, "but he's been away all evening. He is so shy and retiring I encourage him to go to an evening class in flower arranging so he can get out and meet people."

As she spoke, the gorilla ambled in, bowed to Tim, and gave Rosa a beautifully arranged bowl of red and white roses.

Of course, Tim stayed for supper. Rosa made him a cup of tea while the gorilla grilled toasted cheese sandwiches.

The cat snacked, the vulture clacked, the wolfhound crunched, the rabbit nibbled, the gorilla and Rosa and Tim gossiped, the pipes under the sink gargled (or gurgled), and the toasted cheese sandwiches sizzled happily on the griller.

The Springing Granny

O

The winter with ice on the edge of its teeth
Blew snow in the sandpit and hail on the heath.
And, sliding through keyholes and any odd cracks,
Ran shivery fingers down everyone's backs.

"Enough!" cried the granny of Sally and Fred.
"I am getting my comics and going to bed.
Outside there is nothing but struggle and storm
And my bed is so comfy and cosy and warm."

So they put her to bed, downy pillows around her.
The winter wind couldn't get near her to hound her.
Said Granny, "The winter is really a strain,
And I'm not getting out of bed ever again."

"I'm worn out and wrinkly and wispy and white,
And nobody takes me out dancing at night.
My spring is all gone, and I grumble and groan!
I'll invent a new spring that's completely my own."

So she painted her sunshade a beautiful blue,
With a big yellow sun and a white cloud or two.
And she fixed it all up so it covered her bed—
A spangle of springtime spread over her head.

Then, dreaming of sunshine and sea on the beach
And bananas in bunches that hung within reach,
She quickly constructed a couple of palms,
Using tattered umbrellas with sticky-out arms.

Next, she painted some butterflies, fixed them on
    wires,
And sent her old coverlet out to the dyers.

They patched up the place held together with string
And dyed it as green as a meadow in spring.

Reclining at ease on her meadowy quilt,
Granny covered the places where soup had been spilt
By embroidering buttercups, crocuses, clover,
Until the quilt burgeoned and blossomed all over.

Then she sighed and lay back, feeling very contented,
Enjoying the strange sort of spring she'd invented—
A primrose-and-pineapple *tropical* spring
Of the kind that would cause any granny to sing.

Every day after lunch (in her satin pajamas),
She dreamed (as she snored) of the sunny Bahamas

Where curling waves lazily broke on the shore,
And pythons and parrots looked in at her door.

It was all right for Granny...but Sally and Fred
Were kept on the run between kitchen and bed.
"Oh, Fred—carry Granny her cake and her tea,
And please rub the liniment into her knee!

And, Sally—run rapidly! Take her a hotty.
Here's one for her feet—oh, and one for her botty!
Take Granny the paper. Be quiet when you play!"
It was up-and-down, up-and-down all of the day.

Granny read all of her comics, ate nuts by the score
(While carelessly dropping the shells on the floor).
"Oh, Fred, sweep them up! Here's a dustpan and
  brush…
But remember she's sleeping! For goodness' sake,
hush!"

Said Sally, "I'm fed up to *here* with this fuss!
There just has to be something in it for us."

"We could trundle her out to the park," muttered Fred.
"There are people who'd *pay* to see Granny in bed."

So the next day, when Granny was having a nap,
(With nutshells and comic books spread in her lap),
Her tropical springtime in boisterous bloom,
Fred and Sally together crept into her room.

They were silent as shadows; they worked with a will
Guiding Granny (and bed) with remarkable skill
Out over the landing, then on down the stairs,
Around the hall table and hatstand and chairs.

Out over the gap where an old step had gone...
They bumped a few times but their granny slept on,

Entranced by a dream in which pineapple ices
Were served on a seashore all scented with spices.

And she dreamed that her singing had made her a
   star—

She had glittery boots, an electric guitar!
Like a rocket at midnight she lit up the dark...
Then she woke with a fright:
  She was out in the park!

And all round her bed, from her head to her feet,
Were the neighbors who lived in the wintertime
    street—
All clapping their hands and beginning to sing
Their rapturous praises of Granny and spring...

A spring to be looked at, and longed for, and *felt*,
A springtime so real that the snow had to melt,

While the sky, which for weeks had been lowering and
   gray,
Was tender and blue as the clouds rolled away.

She was suddenly famous! A tourist, so keen,
Was making a video of the whole scene,
While TV directors with cameras and crews
Were clustered around shooting scenes for the news.

"Hey, Fred!" muttered Gran. "Make the most of this
   chance,
If you charge them all extra this granny will dance.
Go get me a helping of fried fish and chips,
And I'll dance a fandango and turn a few flips.

"I slept through the winter, but now I'll get up.
For I'm feeling as fresh and as fit as a pup.
The world is so full of remarkable things,
It is spring in my bed...and my bed's full of springs.

"I'll spring till the spring springs. When springtime is
   sprung,
I'll still keep on springing although I'm not young.
And I'll prove to the folk who come flocking to see
That there's nothing but spring in a granny like me."

So she sprang and she sprang, springing higher and
    higher,
She sprang like a lark, or a flame of the fire...
And winter retreated, the morning turned pearly,
And springtime arrived a full week or two early.

Margaret Mahy

grew up in Whakatane, New Zealand, and received a B.A. from the University of New Zealand and a diploma of librarianship from the New Zealand Library Association. After working as a children's librarian for a number of years, she now writes full time and has created a wide range of books, including picture books, collections of verse and short stories, and young adult novels. She has twice won the prestigious Carnegie Medal in England, in 1982 and 1984, for *The Haunting* and *The Changeover*, both published by McElderry Books. Other Mahy titles for young readers include *Nonstop Nonsense*; *The Blood-and-Thunder Adventure on Hurricane Peak*; *Keeping House*; *Making Friends*; and *A Tall Story and Other Tales*, all McElderry Books. Ms. Mahy lives in New Zealand, in a house overlooking Governor's Bay. She has two daughters.

DATE DUE